First edition, 2016

Written in Havana by Matt Glover

Illustrated in Argentina by Gaby Araujo.

Illustrated in London by Lauren Mortimer.

Printed in USA.

For Jackson

Happy reading ☺

Charlie

This Charlie Parris book now belongs to...

YOU!

Thanks so much!

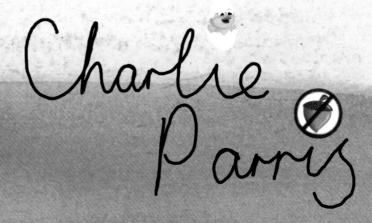

Charlie Parris

Special thanks to Gaby and Lauren
for bringing my crazy story to life
with their excellent illustrations!

I couldn't have done it
without you guys!

Mark
the
Shark

Mark the shark
Came out of the sea,

He said hello to you,
Then said hello to me.

Mark the shark
Went to the park,

He played on the swing,
What a very strange thing!

A shark in the park!
That cannot be!

Mark the shark
Stayed in the park,

He played with a ball,
That makes no sense at all!

A shark in the park!
That cannot be!

Mark the shark
Stayed in the park,

He slid down the slide,
His smile toothy and wide.

A shark in the park!
That cannot be!

Mark the shark
Stayed in the park,

He sat on the see-saw,
But he needed one more.

A shark in the park!
That cannot be!

Mark the shark
Stayed in the park,

He nearly got stuck,
On the fun bouncy duck!

A shark in the park!
That cannot be!

Mark the shark
Stayed in the park,

He whizzed round and round,
On the merry-go-round.

A shark in the park!
That cannot be!

MARK THE
SHARK!
GO BACK TO
THE SEA!

Mark felt a bit dizzy
So went back to the sea,

He said goodbye to you,
Then said goodbye to me!

Mark's all tired and sleepy,
In his sea-bed so blue,

He said goodnight to me,
And goodnight to you.

Fin

How many other Charlie Parris stories have you read...?

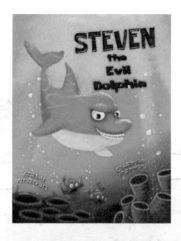

About the author

Charlie Parris is not even French!
He's a story-telling kindergarten teacher from England.
He loves writing children's stories, and can speak over
a dozen languages, including English, Scottish, Irish,
American, Australian, Canadian, Spanish, Venezuelan,
Colombian, Panamanian, Argentinian,
Cuban and Geordie.

Coming soon. . .

Made in the USA
Columbia, SC
25 October 2018